10574110

Jefferson County Library
620 Cedar Avenue
Port Hadlock, WA 98339
(360) 385-6544 www.jclibrary.info

DATE

123 versus ABC

For my wife, Natalie, who is #1 and A+ in my book

123 versus ABC. Copyright © 2013 by Mike Boldt. All rights reserved. Printed in the U.S.A. No part of this book may be used or reproduced in any manner whatsoever without written permission except in the case of brief quotations embodied in critical articles and reviews. For information address HarperCollins Children's Books, a division of HarperCollins Publishers, 10 East 53rd Street, New York, NY 10022. www.harpercollinschildrens.com
Library of Congress Cataloging-in-Publication Data is available. ISBN 978-0-06-210299-7
The artist used Corel Painter to digitally create the illustrations for this book.
Typography by Dana Fritts. 13 14 15 16 17 LP 10 9 8 7 6 5 4 3 2 ❖ First Edition

Mike Boldt

versus ABC

HARPER
An Imprint of HarperCollinsPublishers

WHAT?!!

No no, there must be a mistake here. This book is about magnificent Numbers! We count and measure and add and subtract!
The mistake is all yours. This book is about lovely Letters! We make up the alphabet so you can spell and read!

About *Letters?* Why would all of us **Numbers** be here if this was about *Letters?*
Numbers in a book. That's laughable. As you can see, we Letters are here as well. In fact, today is Bring Your Lowercase to Work Day. Here's little a.

Numbers!
Letters!
Numbers numbers
NUMBERS!
Letters letters
LETTERS!

Umm . . . hello?

Can I help you? Perhaps you need to count something.
Letter A at your service. Do you need assistance spelling something?
LETTERS
I'm not sure. I'm just the one Alligator who was asked to be in this book.

That settles it then. Since there is 1 Alligator, this is a book about Numbers.

Did you hear what you said? Alligator. That starts with the letter A. Just look who else is showing up now.

Bears. B!
2 of them. They arrived in those 3 Cars.
Cars. Which Letter does the word Car start with again? Oh yeah. C.

ICE CREAM

Now look! This is getting better for us Letters. After C comes D and E, right? Those would be Dinosaurs carrying—
4 Dinosaurs carrying 5 Eggs. Followed by 6 toads . . . and . . .
You mean FROGS!
. . . 7 hungry Geese eating those 8 Hot dogs and 9 Ice-cream cones.

a, b, c, d, e, f, G(Geese)! H(Hot dog)! I(Ice cream)! And what's that? A Jigsaw puzzle being put together by Koalas and Lions.
A 10-piece Jigsaw puzzle being put together by 11 Koalas and 12 Lions. Why don't you just quit? Then you won't have to count those 13
Monkeys
wearing 14
Neckties
and juggling 15
Oranges

and the 16 Pigs
and the 17 Queens

18
Robots wearing Sombreros
19 sombreros actually,

20
Turtles

21 Unicycles
with
22 Violins
being played by
23 Wolves
who are also playing all
24 of those
Xylophones!

This is getting ridiculous.
I agree. Why would anyone need 25 balls of Yarn?
To knit sweaters for those 26...

Zebras!!!

Of course. This is a book about Numbers . . .
1 2 3 4
11 12 13 14
20 21 22 23
Aa Bb Cc Dd Ee
Ii Jj Kk Ll Mm
Rr Ss Tt Uu Vv

5 6 7 8 9 10
15 16 17 18 19
24 25 26
. . . and Letters!
Ff Gg Hh
Nn Oo Pp Qq
Ww Xx Yy Zz

Well, it's sorted now at least.
What do you say we call it a day?

Umm . . . hello?
I'm a little lost. I'm
supposed to be in a
book about colors.